17 Things i'm not allowed to do anymore

For Theodora —J.O.

For my cousin Geoff,
who always made me laugh —N.C.

Text copyright © 2007 by Jenny Offill
Illustrations copyright © 2007 by Nancy Carpenter

This is a work of fiction. Names, characters, places, and incidents either are the product of the author's imagination or are used fictitiously. Any resemblance to actual persons, living or dead, events, or locales is entirely coincidental.

Published in the United States by Schwartz & Wade Books, an imprint of Random House Children's Books, a division of Random House, Inc., New York.

SCHWARTZ & WADE BOOKS and colophon are trademarks of Random House, Inc.
www.randomhouse.com/kids
Educators and librarians, for a variety of teaching tools, visit us at
www.randomhouse.com/teachers

Library of Congress Cataloging-in-Publication Data
Offill, Jenny.
17 Things I'm not allowed to do anymore / Jenny Offill ; illustrated by Nancy Carpenter.
p. cm.
Summary: A young girl lists the seventeen things she is not allowed to do anymore, including not being able to make ice after freezing a fly in one of the cubes.
ISBN: 978-0-375-83596-4 (trade) — 978-0-375-93596-1 (lib. bdg.)
[1. Behavior—Fiction.] I. Title. Seventeen things I'm not allowed to do anymore. II. Carpenter, Nancy, ill. III. Title.
PZ7.O327Zv 2006
[E]—dc22
2005016414

The text of this book is set in Regula. To achieve the mottled look, the type was printed onto paper, which was then rescanned and manipulated in Adobe Photoshop. The type was then rescanned and manipulated in pen-and-ink and digital media. The illustrations are rendered in pen-and-ink and digital media. Book design by Rachael Cole

PRINTED IN CHINA
10 9 8 7 6 5 4
First Edition

17 Things i'm not allowed to do anymore

JENNY OFFILL

pictures by
NANCY CARPENTER

schwartz & wade books · new york

I had an idea to staple my brother's hair to his pillow.

I am not
allowed
to use the
stapler
anymore.

I had an idea to glue my brother's
bunny slippers to the floor.

I had an idea to tell
my brother he'd soon
be eaten by hyenas.

I am not allowed to tell my brother's fortune anymore.

I had an idea
to walk backward
all the way to school.

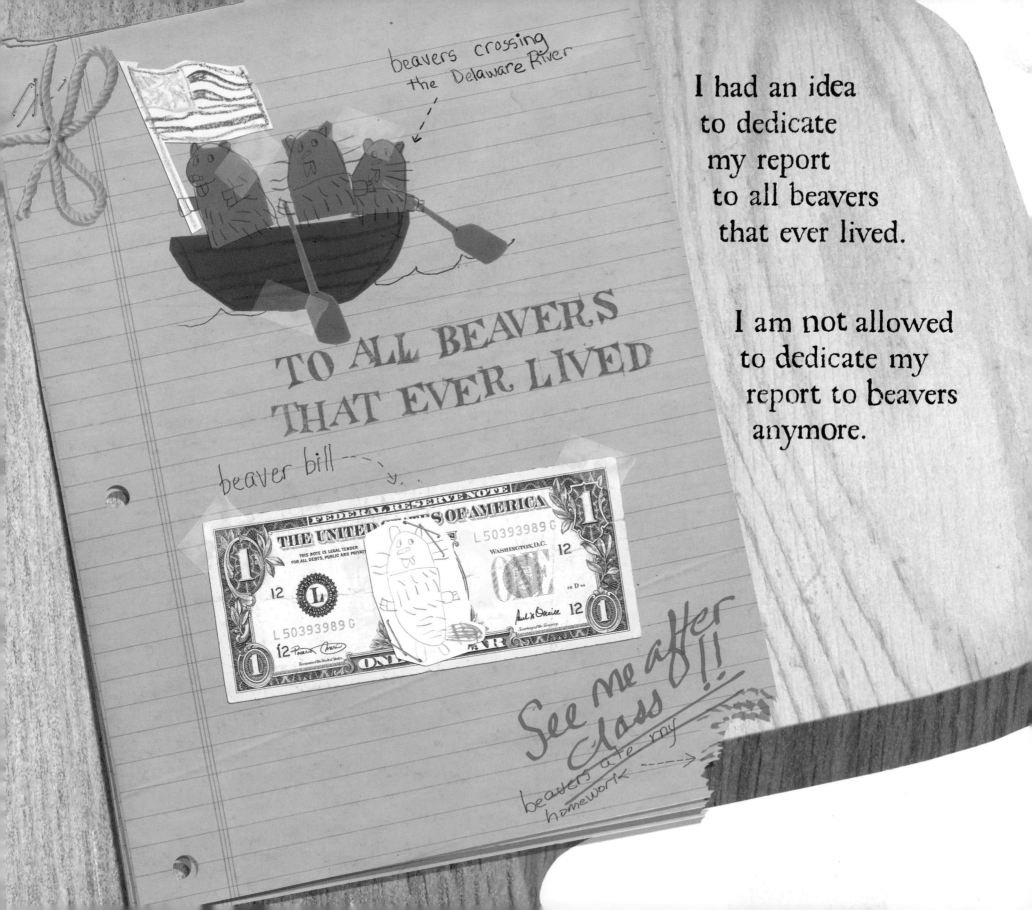

beavers crossing
the Delaware River

I had an idea
to dedicate
my report
to all beavers
that ever lived.

I am not allowed
to dedicate my
report to beavers
anymore.

TO ALL BEAVERS
THAT EVER LIVED

beaver bill

See me after
class!!

beavers ate my
homework

I had an idea to tell the class
I personally owned a hundred beavers.

I'm not allowed to say
that I own beavers anymore.

I had an idea to show Joey
Whipple my underpants.

I am not allowed to show Joey Whipple my underpants anymore.

I had an idea to set Joey Whipple's
shoe on fire using the sun
and a magnifying glass.

I had an idea to walk backward
all the way home from school.

I am not allowed to walk backward home from school anymore.

I had an idea
to wash my hands
in the dog's bowl
before dinner.

I am not allowed
to wash my hands in
the dog's bowl anymore.

I had an idea to give my brother the gift of cauliflower.

I am not allowed to give the gift of cauliflower anymore.

I had an idea to tell the sad story
of a mother who fell into a volcano.

I am not allowed to
tell sad stories about
volcanoes anymore.

I am not allowed
to pretend I've been
struck deaf anymore.

NOT

PRETEND

DEAF

ANYMORE (AGAIN)

I had an idea that I might run away to live with the kind and happy beavers.

I am not allowed to talk (even a little bit) about beavers anymore.

I had an idea to say the opposite of what I mean to trick everyone.

I'M SORRY

I am allowed to say the opposite of what I mean forevermore.